# This Topsy and Tim book belongs to

_____

# Topsy and Tim
# Move House

## By Jean and Gareth Adamson

Illustrations by Belinda Worsley

A catalogue record for this book is available from the British Library

Published by Ladybird Books Ltd
A Penguin Company
Penguin Books Ltd., 80 Strand, London WC2R 0RL, UK
Penguin Books Australia Ltd., 707 Collins Street, Melbourne, Victoria 3008, Australia
Penguin Group (NZ) 67 Apollo Drive, Rosedale, North Shore 0632, New Zealand

002

ISBN: 978-0-72329-258-6
Printed in China

www.topsyandtim.com

Topsy and Tim were going to move house. There was
a lot of work to do before the removal men came.
"We must sort out the things we want to keep and the
things we can throw away," said Mummy.

Dad took down all the curtains. Then he took up the rug. That was a dusty job!

"We'll sort which toys we want to keep and which toys we can take to the charity shop," said Tim. They packed their own toys and books into big cardboard boxes.

Roly Poly and Kitty kept getting in the way.
"Will our pets come with us?" asked Topsy.
"Of course they will," said Mummy.

The removal people came in an enormous van. They were cheerful and friendly but they wasted no time. Topsy and Tim watched them packing things into boxes and putting the furniture into the van.

It should have been fun, but Topsy and Tim grew
sadder as their old home grew emptier.

Soon, the old house was quite empty.
"Time to put the pets in the car and follow the van
to our new home," said Dad.

Topsy carried Kitty in her travelling basket. Tim carried Tubby mouse in his cage and held on tight to Roly Poly's lead. Dad carried the goldfish and Mummy took Wiggles, the rabbit, in a cardboard box.

Kitty got fidgety when the car began to move.
Tim thought she needed a cuddle. He didn't want
to wait until they were at the new house, so when
the car came to a stop on the driveway,
Tim opened the basket.

As soon as he did, Kitty sprang out. Before anyone could stop her, she was out of the car window and away.

Mummy, Dad, Topsy and Tim looked everywhere
for Kitty. They could not find her anywhere.

"It's no good," said Dad. "We need to start
unpacking our belongings in our new home.
We can look for Kitty later on this afternoon."

At the new house, the removal people began to take in
all the belongings. Mummy and Dad asked Topsy and Tim
to help, but they were too upset about Kitty.

Their new next-door neighour made a lovely
surprise picnic tea. But nothing could cheer up
Topsy and Tim.

"I've had a bright idea!" said Dad. He drove away
in the car. Mummy was not very pleased with him.
There was such a lot to do.

Topsy and Tim went out to explore their new garden.
"Let's climb that tree," said Tim.

But Topsy was not speaking to him because
he had let Kitty out.

Suddenly, Dad came back.
"My bright idea was right," he said.
"Kitty had gone back to the old house."

Mummy rubbed some butter on Kitty's paws.
Then she made a safe, cosy cat-bed.
"By the time Kitty has licked that tasty butter off her
paws, she will be feeling at home here," said Mummy.

"Come on, Tim!" said Topsy.
"Let's climb that tree in the garden."

That night, Topsy and Tim slept in their new bedrooms
for the first time.
"Good night. Sleep tight," said Mummy.
Just before Topsy fell asleep, something heavy landed on her bed.
"Hello, Kitty," she whispered.
Kitty purred very loudly. Soon, everyone was fast asleep
in their new home.

*Now turn the page and help
Topsy and Tim solve a puzzle.*

Topsy and Tim are packing away their toys.
Look at the items in the panel opposite and
see if you can find them all in the big picture.

shoebox

block

rabbit

piggy bank

roller skate

# A Map of the Village

farm

Kerry's house

Tony's house

park

garage

post office

health centre

church

primary school

nursery school

police station

# Have you read all the Topsy and Tim stories?

 The New Baby · Jean and Gareth Adamson — 9781409300564

 Have a Birthday Party · Jean and Gareth Adamson — 9781409300618

 Go on an Aeroplane · Jean and Gareth Adamson — 9781409300571

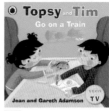 Play Football · Jean and Gareth Adamson — 9781409303350

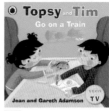 Go on a Train — 9781409304241

 Learn to Swim · and Gareth Adamson — 9781409300601

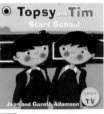 Start School · Jean and Gareth Adamson — 9781409300830

 Go Camping · Jean and Gareth Adamson — 9781409303336

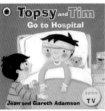 Go to Hospital · Jean and Gareth Adamson — 9781409304234

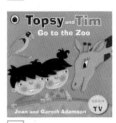 Go to the Zoo · Jean and Gareth Adamson — 9781409300847

 Go to the Dentist · Jean and Gareth Adamson — 9781409300588

 At the Farm · Jean and Gareth Adamson — 9781409303367

 Go to the Doctor · Jean and Gareth Adamson — 9781409303343

 Have Itchy Heads · Jean and Gareth Adamson — 9781409307204

 Meet the Firefighters · Jean and Gareth Adamson — 9781409307211

 Safety First · Jean and Gareth Adamson — 9781409308829

 Meet the Police · Jean and Gareth Adamson — 9781409308836

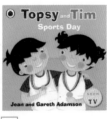 Sports Day · Jean and Gareth Adamson — 9781409309468

 Visit London · Jean and Gareth Adamson — 9781409309475

 Meet Father Christmas · Jean and Gareth Ad — 9781409311591

 Help a Friend · Jean and Gareth Adamson — 9780723292593

 Move House · Jean and Gareth Adamson — ✓ 9780723292586

The Topsy and Tim app is now available

 Available on the App Store

 ANDROID APP ON Google play

The Topsy and Tim ebook range is available through all digital retailers.